Indulge in Love, Healing and You

Indulge in Love, Healing and You

LAQUINTA CLACK

ReadersMagnet, LLC

Indulge in Love, Healing and You
Copyright © 2024 by Laquinta Clack

Published in the United States of America

Library of Congress Control Number: 2024919894
ISBN   Paperback: 979-8-89091-709-6
ISBN   eBook: 979-8-89091-710-2

All rights reserved. No part of this publication may be reproduced, stored in a retrieval system or transmitted in any way by any means, electronic, mechanical, photocopy, recording or otherwise without the prior permission of the author except as provided by USA copyright law.

The opinions expressed by the author are not necessarily those of ReadersMagnet, LLC.

ReadersMagnet, LLC
10620 Treena Street, Suite 230 | San Diego, California, 92131 USA
1.619. 354. 2643 | www.readersmagnet.com

Book design copyright © 2024 by ReadersMagnet, LLC. All rights reserved.

Cover design by Jhie Oraiz
Interior design by Dorothy Lee

Table of Contents

Breakthrough 7
A Mother's Prayer 8
It Will Hurt Later 9
Change Within 10
Where Did Everyone Go? 11
What's Down There? 12
Bloody Heart 13
Love 14
Soul Ties 15
I Gave It All I Could 16
Last Warning ⚠ 17
First Love ♥ 18
A Young Mother 19
I Am 20
Fys (F@$K Your Sorry) 21
The Dark Spot 22
No 23
Access Denied 24
Bullet Proof 25
The Chance To Live Again 26
Him 27
Wounds Into Wisdom 28
My Own Rider 29
Finding My Way Out 30
Another Chance At Love 31
Whatever Didn't Work 32
Never See Me Cry 33
God's Love 34
I Thought I Needed You More 35
My Inner Child 36

Breakthrough

I have to go through to get up
I have to feel the fire in order to enjoy the cool
I have to go through for a breakthrough!
My back maybe against the wall and all odds maybe against me but I'm willing to go through.
People may call me names and throw dirt on me to bury me, but I must go through.
My heart may get broken
My soul may get low at times
My spirit may even feel like throwing in the towel but I must go through.
You won't enjoy your breakthrough UNTIL you go through.

A mother's prayer

When I first felt your kick it felt amazing and I knew it would be a new chapter for me once you got here so I had to change my ways.

Seeing you grow into a man I knew I had done my job and all the times I hit my knees to pray about you they all came to pass. You're an amazing man your caring and your heart is pure. Those characters alone I knew I didn't have to worry any more.

Now that I'm no longer here in the physical I will always be in your heart and even though it's filled with pain right now I'll still be praying here to ask God to heal your heart and I hope you Never tell me Goodbye because I will see you later.

Love, momma

It Will Hurt Later

So much inside
But no outreach
Held it in so long I've became numb
It's only getting worse but my smile shows I'm getting better
Holding the pain in only look good on the outside but on the inside I've died a thousand times
I need to let it out and just scream it didn't hurt in the beginning but it will hurt later!!!

Change Within

With change comes pain
It requires you to become uncomfortable
What I use to love disgust me now
Who I use to like I no longer want to be around
My mindset has changed
My surroundings has changed
My heart has turned and I'm now being who I'm destined to be and not who they wanted me to be
I had to change within for others to see a change in me!!!

Where did everyone go?

As I look around I see that everyone has disappeared!
When I had it all they were all here
Now that my health is bad and I don't have any money,
they've left me!
Sitting here all alone no one to call on
Where have everyone gone?
I'm here when they need me
Mentally, physically, emotionally and spiritually!
I would do all I could just to make them smile but what about me
Where have everyone gone
My love and loyalty was real but I see there is no one here for me.
I have to wipe my own tears and face my own fears,
even when I was there to help them through theirs.
As I sit and look around, I wonder where did everyone go?

What's down there?

Why do you walk around with your head down?
What's down there?
Maybe it's your self-esteem or your confidence!
Pick your head up there's nothing down there for you.
Your crown won't stay on your head that way No one can see your pretty face, with your head hanging down.
What's down there?
Build your confidence
Love on yourself
And quit walking around with your head hanging down,
because there is nothing down there!

Bloody Heart

Wearing my heart on my sleeve, caused my heart to bleed.
I show more love than I receive, caused my heart to skip a beat.
Following my heart, caused it to be damaged. OH Girl!
Pick your heart up.
You've allowed your heart to be stepped on and bruised,
all for the glory of love.
Pick your heart up
Heal your feelings
Apply some pressure, to stop the bleeding
A bloody heart ♥

Love

Love is not a feeling it's an action
How someone treat you shows how much they
love you
Love is built not given
It can sometimes be taken advantage of,
showing too much love can cause hurt.
So many people love to use the word but don't know how to show it!
Don't miscarry your love, make sure you deliver it.
Love is more than just a four letter word, it's the most misused word.
Careful who you give your love to cause they
might just cause you to miscarry!

Soul ties

Soul ties are usually made when his soul takes mine!
From that point on there will be a bond made,
and I will soon feen for his presence.
My legs may start shaking, I may continue to lick my lips just
by thinking about this feeling. I may feel empty the longer I go
without getting the craving I desire.
He don't know when he left he took my soul with him and left his
residue here with me. Now I'm feeling like I need him and he's ok
to go without me just a lil longer than I am.
Soon he will feel like he need to
rejuvenate, because he's gone so long without my touch,
my smile, my presence, and his residue.
That day has came and we have tied the knot
of our souls once again.

I gave it all I could

I cooked, I cleaned, I did what he asked of me.
Whenever he was down, I would be the one lifting him up. when he start hurting, I ran his bath water and even took the extra mile to wash him up, and afterwards gave massages.
I did all this and still I felt unappreciated.
After he cheated and lied to me, I forgave him, and left it there.
I would always protect and defend his name when he wasn't around.
I would give him my last, without him knowing it was my last.
After I GAVE IT ALL I COULD, I still felt unappreciated.

Last Warning

You thought you were playing me.
I can't lie and say you wasn't good at the game.
Time after time I warned you I would leave, but you thought I loved you too much to let
go.... but I warned you.
Every time I would have one foot out the door you did something to make me stay. *sigh* I failed for it again.
Week after week you had something up your sleeve so why not just let me leave?
You said you love me, but love don't hurt.
I warned you!
I paid attention to the small changes:
Leaving early
Less kisses
Different scents
Lack of attention
More arguments.... should I go on?
I promise this time when I leave I'll be gone for good, your sweet talking and pleading won't work. I'm fed up and I'm done. You never thought I'll have the strength to leave and be done for good, but.... I WARNED YOU!!

FIRST LOVE ♥

holding this feeling in got me want to break loose not keeping you i'll feel like a fool when i look deeply in your eyes i go on a journey walking in my shoes i don't think you can handle that but loving me you do a good job at that my pain i show no sign but my heart isn't silent or my mouth isn't closed i just don't show having you as my love i feel like him above but our struggles got me pullin on a rope like a game of tug a war love is a sweet thing but it's also a fearful thing giving you my heart was the scariest thing but it felt good i want to feel like your queen you said ill always have your crown now as i break through i know I found love

A Young Mother

Most young mothers are left alone because a BOY who thought he was a MAN decided to leave her because he thought having a child was too much or it's to early for him to have kids but he wasn't too young for sex or too young to not wear a condom, but just a child. Now the young lady is left alone to take care of a child now she has to think about do she want to keep the child or give it up for adoption to give the child a better life. A young strong woman is going to do all that she can to take care of her child no matter what the circumstances, but a young woman that's still stuck in her ways will not think down the line but only at that moment. She might make the wrong decision and regret it later. A young lady who decides to keep her babies and deal with it whether the father is there or not is more than a young mother she's a smart lady because she knew she would need her baby more than her baby needed her.

I AM

I am not my skin I am much more than that. I am phenomenal in my own way, the lord has made me unique.

I am beautiful, strong, and courageous I am a woman of God I shall receive everything the Lord has for me.

I am not just a mother I am much more than that, I have to define ME!! My strengths are within me and I will bring them out I will be ME!!!
I am who I am!!

FYS (f@$k your sorry)

You have constantly hurt and abused me and I've repeatedly
forgiven you without an apology given.

You thought I would never leave because of my love for you, but
once I realized my love was unconditional but my presence didn't
have to be I decided to leave.

Now that you see that I have walked out you want to straighten up
and apologize, begging on your knees for me to stay,
but it's too late.

My heart has turned cold, my feelings are dead,
and my mind and heart are finally on
the same page, so f@$k your sorry!!

The Dark Spot

On November 8th the day I'll never forget. It felt like my heart stopped for approximately 10mins. Everything this man was saying on the other side of the phone was muffled, my vision blurred and my soul shattered!

My sister was gone and never coming back, so how do I live without her smile, love, and spirit? How would I live day after day knowing I have other siblings that may cause me this pain or worse!!

Some days I wake up happy knowing that your in a better place, because since you left things have gotten worse down here. Other days I wake up screaming at the top of my lungs but not even a sound comes out. Some days I can't help myself but to sit and cry and cry and pray and ask myself why?

Funny how grief works because you still have trouble with letting go of someone who is no longer here!!

No

No I can't be your peace
Though I'm a peacemaker I can't be your peace from all the damage you've cause me all the pain you put me through, No

I can't be your peace because deep down inside your still longing for that mother's love and touch.
I can't be your mother and your love.
When you came to me you should've already been a man, but you were a lil boy at heart with a boy mentality just trapped in a grown man's body, so No!!

I've been your hero too long I've covered all your wrongs, I've treated you like a king even placing you on a throne. We've had sex, made love, but let's be honest that was just your guilt trip from the nights before!!! So no Please don't come looking for me to be your peace because I've found the piece in me that
I've longed for and I can't give my piece of
peace away!!!

Access Denied

You can be in my presence but I won't let you in my heart again!!

I gave you trust, love, and affection and you abused it
Now that I know that game is going to always be same
I'd rather be alone than to be played with so Access denied you'll never get the same me

Bullet Proof

My heart is so fragile
It's already been broken so many times I've built walls of all kind around it, but yet it's gotten bruised.
This time when I wipe my own tears and pick myself up I'll make sure it's bulletproof so I
can't get hurt by you!!

The Chance to Live Again

2corithians 5:8 briefly say we are confident I say and willing rather to be absent from the body, and to be present with the Lord.

I had to leave to live again
Though my time may have seemed short it's not over. I will live again.

The word is yet true that God is the beginning and the end…the end had to happen so a new beginning can come.

I will no longer have to exist but I will Live.

God has called my name and I responded to the call of an everlasting LIFE!!

Here in heaven with our Father I Am living again.

So dry your eyes and praise that another faithful servant has made it a chance to Live again.

-From that special someone

HIM

His kisses make me weak
Whispering sweet nothings in my ear make my
heart skip a beat
The way he walk and talk make me want to risk it all
But I know I'll just get played like a game of basketball
He said he love me, I'm not sure of how true....my heart says go for
it but my mind tells me all niggas are the same
So I'm contemplating on which way to go. If I choose my heart
I'll be blind to love. If I go with my mind I'll love with no
expectations...but deep down I don't want to
be right.
I want to be soft and feminine and let this man lead
I'll cook, clean, and keep up my hygiene While he provide, cherish,
and love on me. That's the kind of man I want....HIM

Wounds into Wisdom

Being young dumb in love I fell for it all
I gave my heart mind and soul just to feel involved
Time after time he showed me I'm not the one
But in my mind i thought I was the only one No boundaries morals or value...being used for what lies beneath...ms. Pretty yea that's what he called it
Love had me getting stepped on walk over and misused...I was so focused on him changing that I couldn't see what was already in front of me.
Now that I put me first and love me more I ended that chapter and closed that door...low self-esteem was no more I raised the bar, fixed my crown, and healed my heart
Now when a new man enter I'll no longer use what I have but know what I'm worth
Turning my wounds into wisdom yea that's
what I call it.

My own rider

I got to ride for me
I'm the driver and the rider
If I have a problem I got me
I'll wipe my own tears while I'm down on my hands and knees, I ask God to send me, ME!!

I'll go to war with anybody about me!
I pat my own back, cause I did it for me! I'm my own keeper, cause when I fall I'll be the one to pick me back up!

I can't keep playing with my own feelings, I can't allow you to play with my heart, Cause I'll be left picking up the pieces. Since I'm the only one who's going to be putting myself back together,
I'll be my own rider, until the wheels fall off, And even after that I'll walk Alone, before I let someone take ME away from ME again!!

Finding my way out

All I know is pain, heartbreak, and shame I sit here and wonder how long is it going to rain.
My mind is full, my heart is heavy I don't know how much more I can carry: from the walk outs, self doubt, and loss..life is just a game of a coin toss from ups and down to feeling abandoned as a child I keep looking to the sky asking God "When are you going to work this out".
They keep telling me to just hold on and
endure but I wonder if they know I can't take it anymore. Im running out of tears and words all I have is a heavy heart that's dragging me to the floor.
ALL I WANT IS OUT!! so I'll do what's required of me through fear, setbacks, and scars I'll stay mindful of every trial and tribulation as I'm on my knees not praying but crawling my way back to me. So if it takes me covering the lies with truth and showing myself love to overcome to self sabotage I have to get back to me, the real me because if I can endure pain I sure enough endure happiness ♥

Another chance at love

Going all in with no regrets
Gave you my heart and I had nothing left My life my love and my time is all I had to offer You promised you wouldn't do me the same
But as time went by I figured you was just running game!
I loved you like nun other I loved you how I wanted you to love me
But I guess that will forever be a dream! All your actions have changed and I've yet remained the same
I took all that you've thrown my way
The dirt, stabbing, and the emptiness
My time here was up but I wanted to be with you more than anything ever, only for you to want someone else
The love I gave you was real and I didn't want to give it to anyone else but you, but I couldn't keep losing myself,
seem as if I was only finding you while you were
trying to push me away.
I've finally found me and He have too.

Whatever didn't work

Past trauma,defeat, and being mislead by the ones that "love" me the most made me
See things differently
I thought I always had a clear view on things until my mind changed and made my vision clearer than before
They say love is blind and I truly believe that because I wanted love and wanted to be loved by friends, family, and the world.
I became a custom to the customs and lived beneath my worth,value, and privilege...I sat in the shadow of others because I didn't see myself. Going through life things kept falling apart no matter how I moved in the things I do it just didn't work.
They say if it's not broken don't fix it...But there was something on the inside of me that I knew was broken cause what I showed on the outside wasn't the me on the inside. And they say what a man thinketh so is He...l knew there was more in me, for me, and on me....
So Now looking back I would like to think whatever didn't work wasn't meant to work and that was God's way of protecting and building me for the things that are Going to work!!

Never see me cry

As a mother and a woman with strong feelings I've dealt with a lot
in my life abuse, rape,
abandonment and more but;
you'll never see me cry.
Behind closed doors I've cried for hours that
might turn into days but I'll go through the day as if there's no rain.
You'll never see me cry.
My children see no one but me this strong woman with integrity.
I'm the one who holds our world together..so though I'm going
through A storm they will never get wet. You'll never see me cry.
Some may call it pride I call it perseverance I had to take what was
given to me and play the
hand I was dealt. It's not that I WON'T complain, I CAN'T,
because I have more than just me that's depending on me:
So you'll never see me cry

God's love

This love is unexplainable, It's such a great feeling.
Unlike man God's love never change
Even when I didn't Love myself He yet loved me and when I came to the realization of His love I can say I don't want it any other way. Someone who love me unconditionally, and He Shows me just How much He love me daily, But the ultimate sacrifice He made just for ME is when He sent His Son JUST to die for ME!! God's Love is like nun other, I'm glad I get to experience a love like this. I once was lost, But God's love found me and helped me love Myself and others. God's love is the reason I'm still here today, without His love I would've gave up A LONG time ago, God's love loved me
back to me!!

I thought I needed you more

I wouldn't call it an addiction but I was addicted to your presence... even though having you around wasn't always pleasant. You bring out the good and the bad in me, you knew just what to do and what to say to push my buttons in a good and bad way.
I knew you wasn't good for me but you were good to me so I wanted to make you the one for me, I was so wrong.
The lack of confidence in myself only brought me to needing validation and you were mine with no hesitation when you came into the room I would light up and my stomach filled with butterflies. My drug when I needed numbing my teacher when I needed help you were my partner in crime, so I thought.
One day that all had changed because I had gained;
My confidence
My self-esteem My worth
I found me and I realized I couldn't love nobody or allow anyone to love me properly if I didn't love me....i honestly thought I needed you here but I realized I needed me more muah

My Inner child

Trying to heal as an adult but was never apologized to as a child, so how can I forgive. They say don't judge your parents, they did the best they could...but I was hurting daily and you didn't notice your child was crying out for love.

I carried so many things into my adult life
- Not know how to love or receive it
- Accepting the bare minimum to have others around
- Crying day and night from past trauma

Wondering will this ever end cause some days
I feel like I'm at my wits end.
If only I was loved properly as a child I wouldn't still be crying out loud as an adult just wanting to be loved.
Or maybe if I got a simple apology I would know how to forgive myself and others

www.ingramcontent.com/pod-product-compliance
Lightning Source LLC
LaVergne TN
LVHW010442070526
838199LV00066B/6152